Little Boy Blue

Little Boy Blue,

come blow your horn.

The sheep is in the meadow.

The cow is in the corn.

But where is the boy

who watches the sheep?

He is under a haystack,

fast asleep.

adapted by Brooke Harris
illustrated by
Gerald Kelley

The sheep is in the meadow.

“Baa. Baa.”

The cow is in the corn.

"Moo. Moo."

Where is Little Boy Blue?

"Yoo-hoo? Little Boy Blue?"

We can look for him in the meadow.

"Little Boy Blue? Where are you?"

We can look for him in the corn.
"Little Boy Blue? Come blow
your horn."

Who will watch the cow now?

Who will watch the sheep?

Look under the haystack.

"Little Boy Blue is fast asleep!"

“Wake up, Little Boy Blue!”

Toot! Toot!